VIKING/PUFFIN

Published by the Penguin Group
Penguin Books Ltd, 27 Wrights Lane, London W8 5TZ, England
Penguin Putnam Inc., 375 Hudson Street, New York, New York 10014, USA
Penguin Books Australia Ltd, Ringwood, Victoria, Australia
Penguin Books Canada Ltd, 10 Alcorn Avenue, Toronto, Ontario, Canada M4V 3B2
Penguin Books (NZ) Ltd, Private Bag 102902, NSMC, Auckland, New Zealand

On the worldwide web at: www.penguin.com

Penguin Books Ltd, Registered Offices: Harmondsworth, Middlesex, England

First published by William Heinemann Ltd 1991
Published by Viking 1999
5 7 9 10 8 6 4

Set in Bembo

Made and printed in Singapore by Tien Wah Press (Pte) Ltd

British Library Cataloguing in Publication Data
A CIP catalogue record for this book is available from the British Library

ISBN 0–670–88627–0

Janet and Allan Ahlberg

The Jolly Christmas Postman

PUFFIN BOOKS

Once upon a Christmas Eve
　　Just after it had snowed,
The Jolly Postman (him again!)
　　Came down the jolly road;
And in the bag upon his back
　　An . . . *interesting* load.

First stop: Four Bears Cottage.

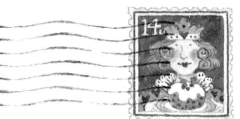

To
Baby Bear
Four Bears Cottage
The Woods

A Christmas card for Baby Bear,
  A babier bear who's shy.
A mummy up a ladder;
  A postman with a pie.
A postman on his bike again:
  Ta, ta! Take care! Bye-bye!

The Jolly Postman cycles on;
  He sees three fiddlers playing;
The fast-eloping dish and spoon;
  The mighty beanstalk swaying;
The seven dwarfs upon the hill;
  The jolly snowmen sleighing.

And, by and by, second stop,
He comes to Red Riding Hood's house.

A jolly game – a lucky girl!
  But see what's written here:
'From Mr Wolf' – he's got a nerve –
  'A Merry Christmas, dear'!
The Postman can't think what to say,
  And sips his ginger beer,

        . . . And eats his pie,
          And waves bye-bye.

The Postman gets back on his bike
  And rides another mile.
A crooked mile, in actual fact,
  It takes him quite a while.
He never finds the sixpence, though,
  Or, come to that, the stile.
And, besides, the crooked man has it.

Next stop: the hospital!

Mr H. Dumpty
Wincey Ward
Cock Robin Memorial Hospital

Humpty Dumpty smiles and blinks.
  'A jigsaw – for me? What fun!' he thinks.
'From all the King's horses
  And all the King's men – how nice.'
Then he falls out of bed
  And gets cracked again, i.e. twice.

Never mind . . .
In comes the doctor (Foster),
In comes the nurse,
In comes the lady with the alligator purse
. . . and they mend him.

The Jolly Postman waves bye-bye;
   He still has far to go.
The sun has vanished from the sky,
   The clouds are hanging low.
He feels a 'kiss' upon his cheek –
   The first fresh flakes of snow.

And comes – number four –
To a small tin door.

PAT O'CAKE
BAKERS
WE USE JOLLY MILLER FLOUR

CROOKED MILE
1 15 PM
22 DEC
1988

THE GINGERBREAD BOY
McVITIE HOUSE
LITTLE TOE LANE
TOYTOWN.

'A book in a book!' says the Gingerbread Boy.
'What a simply *delicious* surprise.'
(But if only he knew, *he's* in one, too –
That really would open his eyes.)
Then . . .
A bucket of tea for the Postman
And four and twenty mince pies.

Off through the snow the Postman rides
 With more than a meal in his insides.
He's all shook up and all of a-quiver,
 And it's not just the cold that makes him shiver.
There's a letter he'd rather not deliver . . .

 To you-know-who.
 Oooooh!

MISTER WOLF

THE
DEN

But all's well and all's merry;
   The Wolf's just wolfing pies and sherry,
And playing games in his cosy den
   ('What's the time, Mr Wolf?')
With the three little pigs
   And the little red hen.

After all, it *is* Christmas.

But now it's *really* snowing,
    And the winter wind is blowing,
And the daylight, it is going.
    So the Jolly Postman – jolly cold –
Has just no way of knowing
    Where he is . . .

He stops beside a wall of ice.
    He spies a crack of light.
He finds a little golden door . . .
    And disappears from sight,
Along a tunnel, dark and cool,
    To a *workshop*, warm and bright.

A cup of tea with Santa,
And Mrs Santa, too.
'Got any *children's* letters?'
The Postman smiles, 'A few!'
'Well, fancy that,' says Santa.
'Now – we've got one for you!'

For our
good old pal
The Postman

Take a Peep!

A peep-show for a postman.
  The Postman peeps inside.
A postman's round completed:
  'It's time to take a ride!'
But how to make the journey?
  The drifts are deep and wide.

To avoid the snow
(Ho, ho, ho!)

p.t.o.

A Jolly Postman, warm and snug.
A postman's dog upon the rug.
A clock that's chiming in the hall.
A *Merry Christmas* – one and all!

The End